WALT DISNEY'S

Cinderella

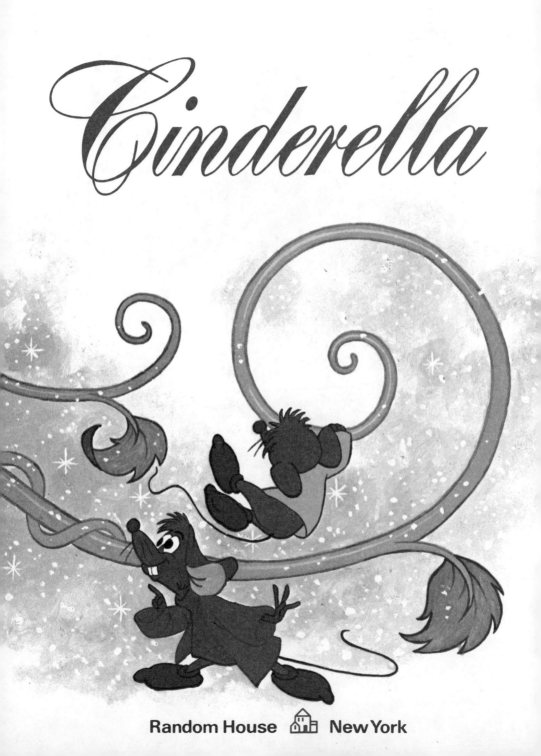

Random House 🏠 New York

Library of Congress Cataloging in Publication Data
Cinderella.   Walt Disney's Cinderella.
(Disney's wonderful world of reading, no. 16)
In her haste to flee the palace before the magic of the fairy godmother loses effect, Cinderella leaves behind one clue to her identity.   [1. Fairy tales.   2. Folklore—France]   I. Disney, Walt, 1901-1966.   II. Title.   PZ8.C488Di3   398.2'1 [E]   73-22325   ISBN 0-394-82552-7   ISBN 0-394-92552-1 (lib. bdg.)
Manufactured in the United States of America

Once upon a time there was a girl
named Cinderella.
She lived with her stepmother.
The stepmother did not like Cinderella.
She made her work very hard every day.

Cinderella had two stepsisters.
Their names were Drizella and Anastasia.

The stepsisters NEVER had to work.
They just pranced around the house
in their fancy dresses.

And they always made fun of Cinderella
because HER dress was so plain.

One day a letter came to the house.

"Drizella! Anastasia!" cried the stepmother. "Listen to this!"

She read the letter. It said:

"The King is giving a ball tonight. His son, the Prince, will choose a wife. Every girl in the kingdom must be there."

"Then I can go, too," said Cinderella.
"YOU!" cried the stepsisters.
And they laughed and laughed.
"But it says every girl in the kingdom must be there," said Cinderella.

The stepmother smiled and said:
"Of course you may go, Cinderella.
You may go IF you do your work first
and IF you have a dress to wear."
"Oh, thank you," said Cinderella.
And she ran up to her room.

Some mice lived in Cinderella's room.
They were Cinderella's friends.
She had even made little clothes for them.
"Guess what?" she cried.
"I am going to a ball at the palace."
"Hooray!" cried the mice.

Then she showed them an old dress.
"It just needs a little mending,"
said Cinderella. "And maybe a sash
and some beads to make it pretty!"
"Yes, yes, Cinderelly!" said the mice.

"CINDERELLA!"
called the stepmother.
Cinderella went downstairs.
"I want you to clean the floor
and wash the windows
and dust the drapes,"
said the stepmother.

"But I did that yesterday," said Cinderella.
"Do it again!" said the stepmother.
Cinderella worked as fast as she could.
But there was always one more thing to do.

"CINDERELLA!"

"CINDERELLA!"

"CINDERELLA!"

"Oh dear," said Cinderella.
"I will never have time
to mend my dress."

"They make Cinderelly
work, work, work,"
said a fat mouse
named Gus.

"She will have no time
to fix her dress,"
said a skinny mouse
named Jack.

"We can do it!" cried the mice.
"We can fix Cinderelly's dress."

Gus and Jack sneaked into a big room.
The stepsisters were dressing for the ball.
"I hate this old sash," said Drizella.
And she threw it down.
"I never want to see these beads again,"
said Anastasia.
And she dropped them on the floor.

Jack grabbed the sash.

Gus picked up the beads.

They took them to Cinderella's room.
"Look! We found these," said Gus.
"Now we can make Cinderelly's dress
REALLY pretty," said Jack.

They measured.
They cut.

They folded.
They sewed.

They worked and worked
as fast as they could.
The hours went by quickly.

Cinderella had to help the stepsisters
with THEIR dresses.

When she was done, the stepmother said:

"It is time to go to the ball, girls.
Are you ready, Cinderella?"

"No," said Cinderella sadly. "I did not
have any time to fix MY dress."

"Too bad!" said the stepsisters.

"You must learn to work faster," said the stepmother.

They watched Cinderella go up to her room.

When Cinderella opened the door,
she saw something wonderful.

Her dress was ready!

"Surprise!" cried the mice.

"It is the prettiest dress
I have ever seen," said Cinderella.

And she put it on.

Cinderella ran down the stairs.

"Wait!" she called. "I can go now.
I have a dress."

The stepmother and the stepsisters
could not believe their eyes.

"My sash!" cried Drizella.

"My beads!" cried Anastasia.

They ripped off the sash
and pulled off the beads.

Cinderella's dress was ruined.

"Come along, girls," said the stepmother.
"The Prince is waiting for you."
　　And off they went to the palace.
　　Cinderella was left behind.

Cinderella ran into the garden.

The mice ran after her.

"How I did wish to go to the ball!"
said Cinderella. "But it is no use.
Wishes never come true."

"Never, my dear?" said a voice.

Cinderella looked up.

There was a little woman with a wand.

"I am your fairy godmother," she said.

"I am here to give you your wish."

"Now let me see," said the fairy godmother.
"I need a pumpkin and a horse and a dog.
What luck! They are right here.
And—ah, yes! I will need some mice."

When the mice heard this, they began to run.
But the fairy godmother stopped them
with her wand.

"Now for the magic words," she said.
"BIBBIDI BOBBIDI BOO!"

She waved her wand.

The pumpkin turned into a coach.

The horse turned into a coachman.

The dog turned into a footman.

And the mice turned into white horses.

"Now hop in, my dear,"
said the fairy godmother.

"But my dress!" said Cinderella.

"Oh, my!" cried the fairy godmother.
"I almost forgot."

She waved her wand again.
Cinderella looked down.
Her dress turned into a white gown.
Her shoes turned into glass slippers.
"Oh, thank you," said Cinderella.

"Now hop into the coach,"
said the fairy godmother.
"But remember! All the magic ends
when the clock strikes twelve."
"I won't forget," said Cinderella.
And off she went to the palace.

At the ball the King was complaining.

"The Prince has met all the girls
in the kingdom," he said. "And he has not
found one he likes."

"Give him time," said the Grand Duke.

"He has had enough time!" cried the King.

Just then Cinderella came into the ballroom.
When the Prince saw her, he bowed.
"May I have this dance?" he asked.
"Yes," said Cinderella.

All night the Prince danced
only with Cinderella.
They danced around the floor
as if in a dream.
Everyone said:
"How lovely she is! Who can she be?"

The hours went by quickly.
Suddenly the clock began to strike midnight.
Cinderella ran down the palace steps.
As she ran she lost a glass slipper.

When the Prince reached the steps,
Cinderella was gone.

He picked up the tiny glass slipper.

"The girl who wore this slipper is the girl
I want to marry," said the Prince.

He told the Grand Duke to find her.

Even before Cinderella was home,
the magic ended.

The coach turned back into a pumpkin.

The coachman turned back into a horse.

The footman turned back into a dog.

And there were Cinderella and the mice—
just as before.

The next day the Grand Duke
took the glass slipper to every house
in the kingdom.

At last he came to the house
where Cinderella lived.

Cinderella was up in her room.

First Drizella tried the slipper.
Her foot was much too long.

Then Anastasia tried the slipper.
Her foot was much too wide.

"Are there any other girls in this house?"
asked the Grand Duke.
"No," said the stepmother.

Just then Cinderella came downstairs.

"Who is this?" asked the Grand Duke.

"She is only the maid," said the stepmother.

"I don't care," said the Grand Duke.

"She, too, must try the slipper."

It fit perfectly!

Then Cinderella reached in her pocket
and pulled out the other glass slipper.
The Grand Duke bowed to Cinderella.
"You are the girl the Prince says
he must marry," said the Grand Duke.

So Cinderella went to the palace
and married the Prince.
And they lived happily ever after.